MR.   BEAR SQUASH-YOU-ALL-FLAT.

STORY BY *Morrell Gipson*

ILLUSTRATED BY *Angela*

FOREWORD BY *Gary Larson*

MR. BEAR

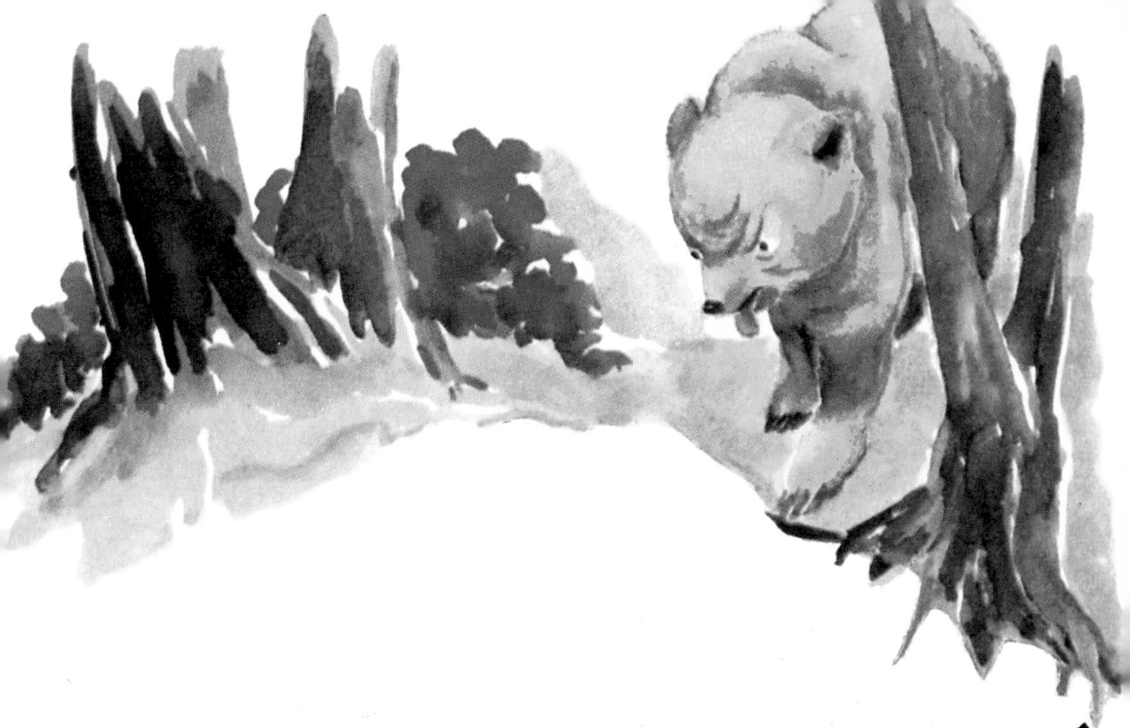

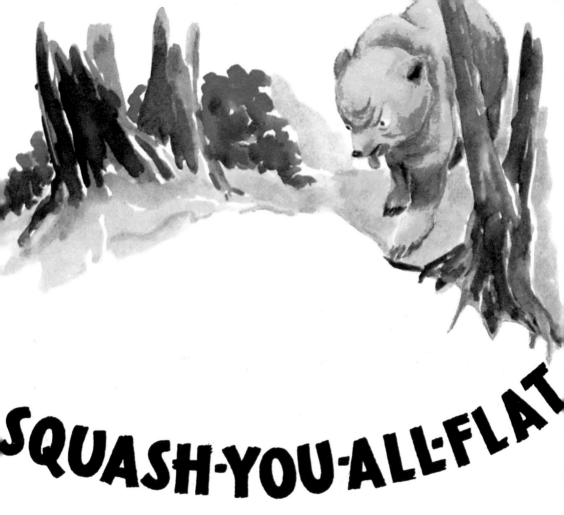

SQUASH-YOU-ALL-FLAT

Purple House Press • TEXAS

Publisher's Cataloging in Publication Data
Gipson, Morrell.
Mr. Bear Squash-You-All-Flat / story by Morrell Gipson;
illustrated by Angela; foreword by Gary Larson. p. cm.
SUMMARY: Mr. Bear, the Neighborhood Nuisance, roams the forest squashing the
houses of other animals – finally getting his own hilarious, smashing comeuppance.
ISBN: 1-930900-04-X
[1. Bears - Fiction   2. Animals - Fiction]   I. 1. Angela 2. Larson, Gary   II. Title
PZ10.3.G46 Mi 2000   [Fic] - dc21 00-107331

A Limited Edition of 250 signed books is available from:
Purple House Press, Ltd. Co., Keller, TX 76248
www.PurpleHousePress.com

Printed in Malaysia
1 2 3 4 5 6 7 8 9 10
First Edition

FOREWORD

Mr. Bear first wandered through my imagination when I was three. And as my mother reminds me today, I absolutely could *not* get enough of the story you now hold in your hands. Every morning, she would sit me down on her lap and read me the exciting tale of this big furry troublemaker with the hilarious last name. "Gary, this was *every* morning," she emphasized, then adding, "and it went on for a long, long time!"

And now, almost half a century later, I have once again sat down with this little book, looking for an answer to the obvious question, "What was up with me and Mr. Bear?" Through the skewed lens of adulthood, could I look back into my early childhood and find the thing in this story that, according to family legend, so gripped my imagination?

Well, my friends, I have been to the belly of the bear, and I believe I may have returned with an answer.

It begins, I'm sure, with the illustrations by Angela. These paintings, if you look closely, are truly from the heart. Her simplicity and relaxed brush strokes are undoubtedly what make this world so accessible to a three-year old.

Ah, but I believe there is something else afoot within these pages. Mr. Bear's scariness — far, far removed from the transparent evil of, say, the Big Bad Wolf — is so softened by Morrell Gipson's gentle humor, that a greater sense of him is fostered. And that is awe. I know I felt it then, I feel it even now. Nothing is more exciting than when Mr. Bear comes "loppety-lop" down some moonlit path. Like all bears, he may seem comical at times, but we know he is also a force to reckon with — in the end, a force that beckons us.

Truth is, as much as I rooted for the other animals in this story (despite what you're thinking), I don't think I wanted Mr. Bear to go away. He, too, belonged in this forest. And I just wanted him to come back. Day after day.

Read it again, Mom.

GARY LARSON

MR. BEAR SQUASH-YOU-ALL-FLAT

Once, in a certain part of the forest, there lived a very large and very stupid bear. His name was Mr. Bear Squash-You-All-Flat. And this is why.

He liked to squash things – he liked to sit on things and squash them flat!

He especially liked to squash the houses of other animals, because he was too stupid to build a house for himself and had to live out of doors all the time.

It is easy to see why this bad habit made him the Neighborhood Nuisance, and why his name was Mr. Bear Squash-You-All-Flat.

For many days Mr. Bear Squash-You-All-Flat would live quietly and peacefully, sleeping under the trees and eating his favorite berries. And then there would be a night when the moon was full, and the next morning Mr. Bear Squash-You-All-Flat would roam over the neighborhood, squashing every house that he saw.

It was lucky for him that he never tried to squash a beehive! But what finally happened to him was almost as bad, as you will find out.

It all began on one of his squashing days, after a very bright full moon had kept him awake the whole night long. He was so cross that he ran loppety-lop through the woods until he came right up to the house of a little gray mouse.

"Hello in there!" he roared. "I am Mr. Bear Squash-You-All-Flat, and I give you fair warning. I am going to count to three, and then I am going to squash-you-flat!"

And he did.

Then, feeling a little better, he shuffled off, looking
for something else to squash.

The little gray mouse, who had run out of harm's way while Mr. Bear was giving fair warning, looked sadly at all that was left of his house. "Ah, well," he said, "no use crying over a squashed house," and started out to find another place to live.

Meanwhile Mr. Bear had come to the home of a chipmunk. "I am Mr. Bear Squash-You-All-Flat," he roared, "and I give you fair warning. I am going to count to three, and then I am going to squash-you-flat!"

And he did.

Now he felt *much* better as he shuffled off, looking for something else to squash.

The chipmunk had heard Mr. Bear coming, and had hidden behind a bush. He gave one low little groan when he saw what had happened to his house. Then he ran away through the woods, looking for another place to live.

By now Mr. Bear had come to another house. It was the home of a baby rabbit who had lost its parents during the last snowstorm of the winter, and who lived all alone. But nothing could stop that stupid Mr. Bear, oh no! He

roared out, "I am Mr. Bear Squash-You-All-Flat, and I give you fair warning. I am going to count to three, and then I am going to squash-you-flat!" And he counted to three, and then he squashed flat *that* house too.

"There, that's enough work for one day," he said to himself. And feeling quite cheerful now, he lumbered off, loppety-lop, to find a shady place where he could catch up on his sleep.

The little mouse was looking everywhere for a new home. He went down a path, and across a meadow, and under a gate, and there –

Right by a brook and in the shade of an oak tree there lay an old tire.

This was not just an ordinary automobile tire. It was a great big super bus tire.

"Why, what a perfectly splendid house," the little mouse said when he saw the tire. "I wonder if it's taken."

He knocked on the tire and called out, "Little house, little house, who lives here?" Not a sound. The mouse looked inside. "Nobody? Then I will."

And he moved in that very day. The next day he repainted all the woodwork.

The next day the chipmunk came scampering along.
He stopped when he saw the tire. "Aha," he said to
himself. "One of those modern houses. And running
water, too." And he called out, "Little house, little house,
who lives here?"

"Nobody but me," answered the mouse, looking out of a window he had just made to catch the morning sun. "Are you looking for a place to live?"

"Oh yes, yes indeed I am," said the chipmunk, giving one great bounce to show that he really meant it.

"Well, come inside then, and let's live together."

And the chipmunk moved right in.

The next morning along came the baby rabbit. He had been lost twice, and was beginning to think that he'd never be able to settle down again, when he saw the old tire. Right away he called out, "Little house, little house, who lives here?"

"We do," said the chipmunk and the mouse, looking out at him. "Come and live with us, if you want to. There's plenty of room for one more."

And so the baby rabbit moved right in. This made the tire quite full, so the mouse hung out a "No Vacancy" sign, and the three of them lived happily together for some time.

Then one night the moon was full and bright, and early the next morning

Loppety-lop

Down the path

Across the meadow

And over the gate

Came that Neighborhood Nuisance, that large and stupid Mr. Bear Squash-You-All-Flat.

As cross as he could be.

The baby rabbit, out getting his breakfast, saw him coming, and ran back to warn the mouse and the chipmunk. They all three hid behind the oak tree, and trembled, and hoped that Mr. Bear would pass by without seeing their house.

But he didn't pass by. He stopped at the brook to get a drink of water, and he saw the old tire.

"Well, well," he said, "*I* think *I'm* going to feel better." And he went right up to the tire, and roared out, "Hello in there! It is I, Mr. Bear Squash-You-All-Flat, and I am going to squash-you-flat."

Just like that, without even counting to three! The baby rabbit hid his eyes. The chipmunk and the mouse sighed. And Mr. bear sat down right on their house, plump!

But nothing happened. That is, nothing happened

except that Mr. Bear bounced, a gentle little bounce into
the air.

    And the tire was the same as ever!

Mr. Bear stood up and looked at the tire. There it was, the same as ever, and not the least bit squashed.

Mr. Bear couldn't believe his eyes. Neither could the three little animals hiding behind the oak tree.

"Perhaps it's because I didn't give you fair warning and count to three," he mumbled. He was such a stupid bear. So he called out, "I am Mr. Bear Squash-You-All-Flat, and I give you fair warning. I am going to count to three, and then I am going to squash-you-flat!" And then he walked a little way off, and came running loppety-lop, and landed plop on the old rubber tire.

And he bounced again. This time he bounced higher.

And there was the tire, the same as ever.

Mr. Bear didn't say a word. He was very, very angry.
He walked 'way away, and then he took a deep breath.
The mouse whispered, "This is it, fellows!" as Mr. Bear
started running faster and faster and faster.

Loppety-loppety-lop

Lop, lop!

And landed on top of the tire with a great thud!

He bounced so high that he banged his stupid head quite hard against the lowest branch of the oak tree, and came down with an awful plop on the solid ground!

There was the tire, the same as ever.

It was quite a shock to Mr. Bear Squash-You-All-Flat. He shook himself once, and felt to see if there were any broken bones. There weren't. And then he ran off, as fast as he could, which wasn't very fast this time.

He never came back to that neighborhood. No matter how bright the moon shone, he never squashed anything any more.

Never again.

As for the mouse, the chipmunk and the baby rabbit —
well, they were so happy that they had to do something.

So they invited all their neighbors to a great big party.

Dear Reader,

When I wrote this story I was living in the country. We had lots of visits from the friendly animals who lived in the woods around us – rabbits, squirrels, chipmunks, deer. But never a bear, thank goodness. I loved our house and our animal neighbors, and I understood very well indeed how bad Mr. Bear was being with his awful squashing habit. So I decided to teach him a lesson he would never forget.

That was a long time ago. My story came out as a book, and it sold and sold until there were no more copies left in the bookstores.

For many years people have been missing Mr. Bear and asking about him. So I was very happy when Jill Morgan of Purple House Press asked me if she could publish my book again. Here it is, with the same wonderful pictures, and with a hope from me that you enjoy it as much as Gary Larson did nearly fifty years ago – and as my granddaughter does today...

Along with a great big BEAR HUG, from

MORRELL GIPSON

PURPLE HOUSE PRESS